UP WITH BIRDS!

John Yeoman and Quentin Blake

PUFFIN
HAMISH HAMILTON

HAMISH HAMILTON/PUFFIN

Published by the Penguin Group
Penguin Books Ltd, 27 Wrights Lane, London W8 5TZ, England
Penguin Putnam Inc., 375 Hudson Street, New York, New York 10014, USA
Penguin Books Australia Ltd, Ringwood, Victoria, Australia
Penguin Books Canada Ltd, 10 Alcorn Avenue, Toronto, Ontario, Canada M4V 3B2
Penguin Books (NZ) Ltd, Private Bag 102902, NSMC, Auckland, New Zealand

Penguin Books Ltd, Registered Offices: Harmondsworth, Middlesex, England

First published by Hamish Hamilton Ltd 1998
3 5 7 9 10 8 6 4 2

Published in Puffin Books 1999
1 3 5 7 9 10 8 6 4 2

Made and printed Italy by Printer Trento srl

British Library Cataloguing in Publication Data
A CIP catalogue record for this book is available from the British Library

ISBN 0-241-13779-9 Hardback
ISBN 0-140-56285-0 Paperback

It was a long, long time ago, several years before you were born, that birds first began to fly. I'll tell you how it happened.

In the days when birds used to walk everywhere life was very difficult indeed. Especially for the Fflyte family who lived in a small town where there were lots of birds. Most of them were very nosy, and whenever they found an open door they would just walk in.

It took Mrs Fflyte hours to run the vacuum cleaner over the carpets because she had to keep switching it off to remove small birds from the nozzle.

It took Mr Fflyte ages to drive his van into the town centre because there would be so many birds walking in front of it. And some of them walked terribly slowly; particularly the penguins.

And the children, Toby and Sophie, often used to have to carry their bicycles over their heads on their journeys to and from the school to stop the birds pecking the tyres.

But things were even worse in the evenings when it started to get dark. Just as birds nowadays like to fly up into the branches of trees to go to sleep, so the birds then always tried to find somewhere comfortable for the night. And quite a few of them regularly stayed at the Fflytes'.

The Fflytes lived above their little shop. Mrs Fflyte made cushions and pillows, which she stuffed with all the loose feathers lying around. And Mrs Fflyte never ran short of feathers.

Mr Fflyte drove his little van about – as best he could – mending things for people.

Late one Friday afternoon Mrs Fflyte looked up as the door bell tinkled. It wasn't a customer, it was Sophie home from school.

"Hello, Mum," she called, "can I have my tea?"

"When you've done your homework," said Mrs Fflyte. "And do close the door, love; you've just let in two herons, and you know how crowded it gets up there in the sitting room."

"Sorry, Mum. I keep forgetting," said Sophie, and she closed the door.

She went up to the sitting room and made some space for herself at the table.

A little later a couple of budgerigars came panting in, followed by a cross-looking stork and Toby. He sat down to work next to Sophie.

But a family of jackdaws under the table kept trying to untie his shoelaces and unpick his socks, and so it was impossible for him to keep his mind on his work.

"I think there are more birds than ever this evening," he exclaimed, slamming the book shut.

"I think there are," sighed his sister, "but there's nothing we can do about it."

"There must be *something* we could do to stop them making such a nuisance of themselves," he said.

Sophie thought for a moment, and then said, "Have you noticed how good they are at holding on to things with their feet? Well, if we fixed up Mum's washing-line across the room we could sit the birds on it."

It was worth a try. While Sophie went on to the little balcony to collect the washing-line, Toby rummaged through their dad's toolbox to find some hooks.

Sophie steadied the chair while he screwed in the hooks all round the walls, and then they strung the line across the room. The birds looked interested.

They didn't seem to mind in the least when Sophie and Toby started picking them up and placing them on the line. In fact, they seemed quite pleased. Even the albatross, which was so heavy that it took the two of them to lift, made no objection.

The penguin was the only one that couldn't get the hang of it. He kept falling off.

When their dad came home and their mum had closed the shop, they all sat down to their tea.

Sophie and Toby explained what they had done, and Mr and Mrs Fflyte were very impressed.

"It makes a nice change not to have birds under your feet all the time," said Mr Fflyte. "If only the streets were as tidy as this."

"Couldn't we do the same out there?" said Sophie. "Couldn't we put all the birds on the telephone wires?"

"They'd never stay still," said Mrs Fflyte. "Not during the day, they wouldn't. They're much too fidgety."

"You'll have to think of something, Dad," said Toby.

His father looked thoughtful and scratched his head from time to time during the meal. And then, when the table had been cleared, he made a few quick sketches on his notepad. Mr Fflyte fancied himself as something of an inventor, and he looked quite pleased when he'd finished scribbling.

"The way I see it," he said, "is that there isn't room for both birds and people on the ground. Now, you two have solved the problem in here by putting the birds in the air. But, as your mother pointed out, that would never work in the street. So that means that when we're outside *we'll* have to take to the air and leave the ground to the birds. See; I've done a couple of drawings."

The other three crowded round his chair, and all the birds craned their heads forward to have a look.

"It's brilliant!" cried Sophie. "Please make one for each of us, Dad. I'm getting so tired of carrying that bicycle to school."

Mr Fflyte got out his toolbox and his odd bits of scrap metal. Toby helped him measure and cut the rods to make some flaps. Sophie helped him glue some material over the flaps to cover them. And they both helped him with the tricky business of joining it all together with string and hinges and springs.

Finally they had four rough-and-ready machines on the living-room floor. There wasn't much space left.

“They’re great, Dad!” said Toby. “How do they work?”

“Well, you sit on the saddle and pedal, just as if it were an ordinary bicycle,” explained Mr Fflyte, “except that you turn these little wheels on the handlebars to make the flaps move.”

“Super!” cried Toby. “Can we have a go now?”

“No,” said Mrs Fflyte. “It’s much too late and it’s much too dark. And, anyway, those ugly old flaps would look much nicer if we decorated them with feathers. We’ve got plenty. The birds have been shedding them like mad in their excitement.”

“Your mother’s right,” said Mr Fflyte. “And in any case, I suspect that the machine might be a bit heavy with all that iron. First thing tomorrow morning I’ll go out and buy a lot of balloons and fill them with gas. Then we can tie them to the air-bicycles for a bit of extra lift.”

“But before you go to bed you can help me glue the feathers on,” said Mrs Fflyte.

The next morning, which was a Saturday, the children woke to find that their dad had been out early to buy the balloons and was hard at work blowing them up. The birds were still there.

"Come and have something to eat," said their mum. "Then we'll go for a spin."

Mr Fflyte had bought far too many balloons. By the time Sophie and Toby had finished breakfast, he had attached about half of them to the machines, and had taken the largest one out on to the balcony.

"I think he might have overdone the gas," said their mum as she watched him struggling to hold the contraption down. "Still, it's better to be on the safe side."

They all went out on to the little balcony to watch. The birds joined them.

"I'll just try it out first," said Mr Fflyte, putting on his crash helmet and goggles. "We'll probably find it very easy once we get used to it."

He sat on the saddle, kicked off with his feet, and rose several feet into the air, pedalling steadily and waving his feathered flaps up and down. The machine stayed still, more or less, hovering just above their heads.

"It's fab!" said Toby.

"It's fun," said Sophie, "but at that rate it'd take days to get to school."

The birds were fascinated, especially the kestrel and skylark.

"It's quite safe," said Mr Fflyte. "Come and join me."

Mrs Fflyte and the children were soon in the air, flapping away and hovering like Mr Fflyte. After a while, Toby discovered that, by turning the handlebars, he could go round in a circle. Soon they were all turning round in circles and getting slightly dizzy, but none of them had any great success in moving forwards.

"What on earth are the birds doing?" called Sophie, pointing to the balcony.

They had all come out of the sitting room, each one holding the string of a balloon in its beak. And they were jumping, one by one, on to the railings.

Then, to the amazement of the Fflytes, they all launched themselves into the air. All, that is, except the penguin, who had second thoughts and went back indoors.

It worked: the birds had taken to the air almost as well as the Fflytes. And they were clearly very excited by the experience.

In fact, one fat sparrow who was floating above Toby's head got so excited that he gave a chirp of pleasure and let go of his balloon. Immediately, he started to fall.

In a panic, the terrified sparrow began flapping its wings wildly, and then, to its amazement, shot upwards again. After that, still flapping, it went round in circles for a while, and then looped the loop.

Finally, it landed on Toby's handlebars,
panting, with a broad smile on its beak.

The result was amazing. At that moment all the other birds let go of *their* balloons and discovered that they could do exactly the same. The sound of ecstatic twittering was deafening.

The news spread like wildfire and soon the skies were filled with birds doing acrobatics. The bolder ones were making dizzy circles round all the tall trees and church steeples. There wasn't a single bird to be found in the streets that morning.

Since the sky was getting as crowded as their sitting room on a cold evening, the Fflytes decided that they'd taken enough exercise for that day, and landed back on their balcony.

Over a cup of tea, they agreed that it had been very extraordinary indeed.

"But it wasn't really a success," said Mr Fflyte. "We weren't getting anywhere."

"Nonsense," said Mrs Fflyte, "we had a lovely time, we taught the birds how to fly and we can all go out together tomorrow afternoon for a real cycle ride."

And they did, and it was sheer joy not to have to keep stopping.

They waved to the sparrows on the gutters,
to the swallows on the telephone wires,
to the jackdaws swirling round the church tower,
and to the vultures on the butcher's roof;
and they arrived home tired but happy.

"Of course it was a success," said Mrs Fflyte.

So Mr Fflyte was pleased. But he and the family were even more pleased when an engineering company bought his invention off him for several hundred pounds. I don't know what they did with it.